TIMEOUT!

HEADS UP, FOOTBALL FANS.

HEAD-TO-HEAD FOOTBALL is a very different kind of book; it can be read frontwards or backwards. Start from one end and you'll get the inside stuff on Detroit Lions' all-star running back, Barry Sanders. Or start from the other side to get the lowdown on the Dallas Cowboys' record-setting running back, Emmitt Smith.

Whichever way you begin, you'll want to read *both* superstar stories before tackling the amazing middle section of the book. See how Emmitt and Barry both overcame their small size to do big things on the football field. Read how, year in and year out, they battle each other for the NFL rushing title. Then check out the fantastic photos, stats, and comic strip that show just how these gridiron greats stack up against each other.

Okay, it's time for the coin toss. So pick Barry or Emmitt and get ready for all of the Head-to-Head action!

CONTENTS

UNSTOPPABLE!

Something was wrong, very wrong, and Emmitt Smith knew it. As the Dallas Cowboy running back got up off the turf, he felt a pain on his right side. It started in his shoulder and spread down his whole arm. Not now, he thought. Not in the middle of the biggest game of the year!

It was the last game of the 1993 National Football League (NFL) regular season. The Dallas Cowboys were playing the New York Giants at Giants Stadium, in East Rutherford, New Jersey. Both teams had a record of 11–4. The winners would clinch first place in their division, the National Football Conference (NFC) East.

The winning team would also earn the right to home field advantage in each of its playoff games. The losing team would still finish with one of the three best records in the (NFC). But it would make the playoffs as a wild card and would have to play an extra game, the following week. Emmitt had something on the line besides the division championship. He was trying to win his third straight NFL rushing title — a feat that had not been accomplished in more than 10 years.

The stage was set at Giants Stadium. During the first half of the game, Emmitt was the star of the show! He carried the ball 19 times for 109 yards. He also caught six passes for another 42 yards. One of those catches was a five-yard scoring reception. It provided the only touchdown to that point in the first half.

His last run of the half was a 46-yard gain that set up a Dallas field goal. During that run, Emmitt got hurt. He had busted through a hole up the middle and was sprinting down the right sideline. Giant safety Greg Jackson made a crushing tackle. Emmitt fell hard, landing on his right arm.

At halftime, the Cowboys were ahead, 13–0. But the mood in the Dallas dressing room was gloomy. The Cowboy medical staff gave Emmitt the bad news: He had a separated right shoulder. That meant the top of his arm had come loose from the shoulder joint.

It wasn't a complete separation, but it was the kind of injury that could put a player out of action for a while. Emmitt didn't want to come out of the game.

"The pain was so bad I couldn't even describe it," he told reporters after the game. "But when Kevin [Dallas trainer Kevin O'Neill] asked me if I wanted to come out, I told him, 'I'm not coming out. I've got to play.'"

The medical crew needed to find a way to protect Emmitt's shoulder and hold it in place. But there was no easy way to do it. They put a harness under Emmitt's shoulder pads and taped a knee pad to his shoulder. Then, they wrapped the whole area with a bandage to keep all the padding together. They helped Emmitt pull on his jersey and sent him out for the second half.

With almost a two touchdown lead, the Cowboys had hoped to let Emmitt watch the rest of the game from the sidelines. That was before the Giants clawed their way back. They kicked a field goal late in the fourth quarter to tie the score, 13-13. When the gun sounded to end regulation play, the score was still tied. The NFC East championship would be decided in sudden-death overtime — a 15-minute extra period in which the first team to score would win the game.

Emmitt's shoulder hurt so much, he could barely move it. As he stood on the sideline, his arm hung stiff and motionless. He wasn't sure if he could even hold onto the ball. But the game was on the line. When the Cowboy offense got the ball in overtime, Coach Jimmy Johnson sent Emmitt onto the field.

In the huddle, Emmitt asked his teammates for a favor: "Guys," he said, "whenever I get tackled, somebody has to help me get up."

Dallas started on offense at its own 25-yard line with just over 10 minutes to play in the overtime period. Emmitt lined up in the backfield behind quarterback Troy Aikman. He took the handoff and ran to his right, gaining two yards. After the play, his offensive linemen helped him get back on his feet. He knew he wouldn't be able to do it on his own.

On the next two plays, Troy passed the ball to Emmitt. Emmitt couldn't lift his arm to catch the ball, so the passes had to be waist high. Both passes were on target and led to a total gain of 17 yards.

On the next play, Emmitt took a handoff and ran the ball for one yard. He was slammed down by Giant linebacker Lawrence Taylor, one of the hardest hitters in pro football history.

The pain caught up with Emmitt. He had to run over to the sideline for a rest. Dallas head coach Jimmy Johnson told him that he didn't have to go back into the game. Emmitt said he would play as long as he could. After the Cowboys ran two plays without him, Emmitt jogged back onto the field.

"You could see he was in pain," said Giant linebacker Michael Brooks after the game. "But he kept on coming. That's a great competitor."

The Cowboys gave the ball to Emmitt five times in a row, and he didn't let them down. He caught a pass for seven yards, ran for three yards, broke another run for 10 yards, and then ran for one more yard. Then he was stopped at the line of scrimmage for no gain.

But by then, Emmitt had carried the Cowboys into field goal range. With just over four minutes left in the overtime, out came veteran kicker Eddie Murray. He would attempt a 41-yard field goal. The kick was good! The Dallas

Cowboys were the NFC East champs!

Despite the pain, Emmitt had had a great day. On the game-winning drive, he handled the football on 9 of the 11 plays leading up to the field goal. In all, he had carried the ball 32 times for 168 yards and caught 10 passes for another 61 yards. He finished with a total of 229 yards!

When his teammates were interviewed by reporters after the game, they could not stop talking about Emmitt.

"I can't tell you the admiration I have for Emmitt Smith," Troy Aikman said. "I see him play every week, so not much surprises me anymore. But that was amazing."

"You can't imagine the courage it took for him to be out there," said wide receiver Micahel Irvin, one of Emmitt's best friends on the Cowboys. "He's the ultimate team guy. He did that for us, because he knew we needed him. We couldn't do it without him."

While his teammates raved about him, Emmitt had his shoulder checked by team doctors. They put his sore arm in a sling.

Afterwards, Emmitt talked to reporters. "You hear all the time about guys playing hurt," Emmitt said. "I wanted to be a guy who could play hurt and be effective."

Emmitt was more than effective. He was awesome. Not only did the game put Dallas in good position to win another Super Bowl, but it gave Emmitt a total of 1,486 rushing yards for the season. That was 57 more than Jerome Bettis of the Los Angeles Rams had. Emmitt had won his third straight rushing title! It was the fourth time in NFL history that a player had won three straight rushing titles. It was the first time it had happened in 13 years.

Sportswriter Michael Wilbon of the *Washington Post* summed up Emmitt's season by writing: "Do we really need to wait for the votes to be counted before we know Emmitt Smith is the most valuable player in the NFL?"

Sure enough, Emmitt was voted the league's MVP. It was just the latest honor for a player who had been doing the impossible on the football field ever since he was a kid.

HEAD TO HEAD

Emmitt Smith and Detroit Lion running back Barry Sanders are the only two players who have won NFL rushing titles in the 1990's. Emmitt won the title in 1991, 1992, and 1993. Barry won it in 1990 and 1994. The record for most seasons leading the league in rushing is eight, held by Cleveland Brown great Jim Brown (1957–61, 1963–65).

BORN
TO RUN

E mmitt Smith was born on May 15, 1969. As a young boy, he spelled his name the way it appeared on his birth certificate, Emmit James Smith III. There was just one "t" in Emmit. But when he entered Brownsville Middle School, his name was spelled wrong. Somebody added an extra "t" to his name. He liked it! From then on, his name was E-m-m-i-t-t.

Emmitt grew up in Pensacola, Florida. It's a small city in northwest Florida, near the border of Alabama. His father, Emmit Junior, worked as a bus driver. When Emmitt was 8, his mom got a job working for a bank. His parents still live in Pensacola today.

Emmitt is the oldest boy in the Smith family. He has three younger brothers. Erik is a year younger than Emmitt, Emory is 5 years younger, and Emil is 10 years younger. He also has two sisters, Marsha and Connie. They are both older than Emmitt.

Family has always been important to Emmitt. When he was growing up, his aunts, uncles, cousins, and grandparents lived nearby. They spent a lot of time together.

Emmitt's grandmother wasn't able to walk, so he and his dad would help her around the house. Emmitt and Mr. Smith washed dishes, vacuumed, dusted, raked leaves, and more. The whole Smith family shared a closeness that Emmitt knew was very special.

"There is nothing that I am today that I would be without family," says Emmitt.

Even as a baby, there were signs that Emmitt would be a football player. When there was a game on TV, Emmitt would rock in his baby swing, with his eyes glued to the set. He loved watching football.

Sports were always a big part of Emmitt's life. His love of sports came from his father, who was a good athlete. Mr. Smith played basketball in college, but he had to leave school early to take care of his sick mother. He also played Dixie League semi-professional football in Pensacola. He was a wide receiver and a safety with a team called the Pensacola Wings.

Emmitt's father never pressured his son to play football. He didn't have to — Emmitt loved the game. As a kid, Emmitt liked the Dallas Cowboys. They were an excellent team and many of their games were shown on TV. Dallas games were also broadcast on radio in 19 different states. Fans from all over the country were able to follow the Cowboys. They were known as "America's Team."

Once, when Emmitt was about 5 years old, he was

watching a game on TV with his father and his cousins. Emmitt was lying down when he announced, "One day I'm going to play for the Dallas Cowboys!" His father and cousins thought it was funny. After all, Emmitt was a just little kid — with a very big dream. They could never have known that someday he really would play for the Cowboys!

Emmitt was a Cowboy fan because he liked their two offensive stars, quarterback Roger Staubach and running back Tony Dorsett. He had been rooting for both of them since he was very young. He liked Roger's leadership skills and "never give up" attitude. Tony was a small runner, who was not afraid to run into the line. Emmitt admired that about him.

When he was 5 years old, Emmitt would play football with his cousins. They were older and bigger than he was, but that didn't bother Emmitt. He often played football, basketball, and other sports with older kids. Emmitt had no trouble keeping up with them. In fact, he was usually the best player in the group. When he was young, he was big for his age. Emmitt finds that funny these days. Why? He's still compared to other players, but now most people think he's small!

Emmitt and his cousins played football in a park near Emmitt's house. This upset his mom sometimes. It wasn't the football part that bothered her — it was the muddy clothes Emmitt would come home in. To keep his mom from getting angry, Emmitt turned his clothes inside-out before he played. He didn't think she would notice dirt on the inside of his clothes. She did!

Emmitt's parents had three main rules for their kids: never break the law; hit the books before playing sports; and always be home before dark. Emmitt rarely broke his parents' rules. He does remember one time when he did. He went to a friend's house to watch movies on TV. When he came home, it was very late. His mother punished him, so he made sure it didn't happen again.

When he was 8, Emmitt played organized football for the first time. He was in the mini-mite division of the Salvation Army Optimists League. His next league was with the Belleview Packers Youth Association League. Emmitt played most of his youth football at Packer Field. It has a new name now— Emmitt Smith Field. Emmitt wore number 45 when he played there. Nobody in the league will wear that number again — it has been retired.

When Emmitt was 12, he got a part-time job working in a nursing home. He mowed the lawn and helped the janitor with odd jobs. Sometimes he would push patients in their wheelchairs. Emmitt used his money to buy new clothes and to play at the arcade.

Emmitt attended Brownsville Middle School in Escambia County, near the city of Pensacola. There he played basketball and ran track, but football was his best sport. His talent caught the eye of Dwight Thomas, the new head coach at nearby Escambia High School.

High school football is very popular in Florida. Some high school games draw bigger crowds than college games. Escambia was not one of those high schools. Its football team had had just one winning season over an 18-year period. Coach Thomas thought Emmitt might help turn things around for their football program.

He liked what he saw in Emmitt, and not just on the field. Coach Thomas remembered meeting Emmitt for the first time, when he was visiting Brownsville Middle School. He was surrounded by a bunch of loud, rowdy kids. But Emmitt was a very polite, well-dressed 14-year-old. He walked up to Coach Thomas and shook his hand: "Hello, coach," he said, "I'm Emmitt."

The next fall, 1983, Emmitt was given a uniform (number 24) and a position on the team. He was the starting running back for the Escambia Gators!

Coach Thomas taught Emmitt and his teammates a lot about football, but he also taught them other things. He made sure his players went to class, studied hard, and kept out of trouble. Emmitt listened to his coach, and he worked hard so that he could succeed on and off the football field.

In the first game of his high school career, Emmitt rushed for 115 yards and two touchdowns. He never let up after that. Twice that season, Emmitt rushed for more than 200 yards in a game! Escambia not only had a winning season in Emmitt's first year, but it advanced to the divisional playoffs.

In his sophomore year, Emmitt helped Escambia to another winning season. He led them to the state football championship on the 3-A level (the second-best level in the state). The next season, Escambia moved up to the AAAA (4-A) level. The 4-A level is the toughest, and the one in which the biggest schools in the state compete. With Emmitt leading the charge, Escambia won that championship, too! During Emmitt's senior year, Escambia was so good that, for six weeks, *USA Today* ranked it as the Number 1 high school team in the country.

Any team that played Escambia knew there was only one way to win the game — they had to stop Emmitt. For one game, the opposing team's defense showed up wearing Emmitt's uniform number on their helmets. They were trying to scare him, to make him think they were out to get him. It didn't work.

Emmitt's running style was based on his great vision. He lined up deep behind the quarterback, so he could get a good running start before taking the handoff. Since his vision was so good, Emmitt could see a hole the second it opened up. And since he had those extra few steps as a head start, he would burst through the hole before anyone could touch him.

"For four years we did three things and won two

state championships doing them," Coach Thomas said. Those three things were "hand the ball to Emmitt, pitch the ball to Emmitt, and throw the ball to Emmitt."

By the time his high school career was over, Emmitt had rushed for 8,804 yards. (Ken Hall is the record-holder for yards rushed in high school, 11,232. Brad Hocker is number two on the all-time list with 9,139 yards. Emmitt's high school total puts him in third place.)

Emmitt scored 106 touchdowns in 49 games, averaging more than two touchdowns per game throughout high school. He rushed for more than 100 yards in 45 of those 49 games. Perhaps the most amazing statistic is this: He only fumbled the ball six times in four years.

Emmitt was a hero at Escambia High School, but he didn't let the success get to his head. He did well in the classroom, keeping up a B average. Math was his favorite subject. He loved fractions and geometry. When Emmitt wasn't playing football or doing his schoolwork, he liked to go to the arcade to play pinball and video games. He also enjoyed fishing with his friends. Emmitt rode his bicycle a lot, too. Sometimes he'd ride 10 miles or more! That exercise helped him become a better athlete.

Emmitt liked helping other kids. He spent a lot of his free time speaking to other teenagers as part of the "Say No to Drugs" campaign. In fact, during the summer before his senior year of high school, Emmitt received a special honor. He was picked to represent all high school football players at a "Just Say No to Drugs" event in Washington, D.C. While he was there, he got to meet one of his sports heroes, Hall of Fame basketball player Julius Erving.

The week before graduation Emmitt spent his free time speaking to students who were in danger of dropping out of school. His parents had taught him the importance of education. He told kids to stick it out and stay in school.

"I have three children, and I just hope they can be like [Emmitt]," Coach Thomas once said. "And I don't mean anything about athletics."

After the 1986 football season ended, it was time for Emmitt to decide where he would go to college. Even with all the records Emmitt had set in high school, some colleges didn't think he was big enough (5' 9" tall and 190 pounds) to be a star on the next level. None of the recruiting services, which grade the best players, listed Emmitt among the top 50 high school players in the nation.

Many schools wanted Emmitt anyway. He accepted a football scholarship to attend the University of Florida. The school had a young football team, so Emmitt thought he would have a good chance of starting as soon as he got there. Plus, his mother wanted him to go there. She thought he would get a good education at the University of Florida. And she liked that the school wasn't too far away from their home in Pensacola.

Even though Emmitt was a big star in high school football, there was no guarantee that he would be a star in college. After all, most of the players on big college teams had been big high school stars.

Emmitt wasn't worried. He had confidence in himself. That confidence came through loud and clear in January 1986. That's when Emmitt got something all football fans want — a ticket to the Super Bowl. He and a friend flew to California, where they saw the New York Giants and the Denver Broncos play in Super Bowl XXI. The Giants won 39–20.

As Emmitt sat in the stands at the Rose Bowl in Pasadena, California, he was one of more than 100,000 fans watching the game. "I'm going to be right there some day," Emmit said to his friend, pointing to the field. "I'm going to be out there playing."

HEAD TO HEAD

The Smith family spent a lot of time at the Escambia High School football field. On Friday nights, Emmitt played his high school games there. On Saturday mornings, Emmitt's brother, Emory, played pee-wee games there. And on Saturday nights, Emmitt's father played for a semi-professional team — on the same field!

3

FANTASTIC
FRESHMAN

Emmitt had to leave home to go to college, but he did not have to leave his home state. The University of Florida is in Gainesville, which is 350 miles (about a seven-hour drive) from Pensacola. His family would have no trouble coming to watch his games.

The University of Florida's athletic teams are nick-named the Gators. They play in the Southeastern Conference. The football team's home stadium is named Florida Field, but fans call it "The Swamp."

There are several former Gators in the NFL today. They include John L. Williams of the Pittsburgh Steelers, Errict Rhett of the Tampa Bay Buccaneers, and Wilber Marshall of the Arizona Cardinals.

In the years right before Emmitt's arrival, Florida had some of its most successful seasons. From 1983 to 1985, the Gators won 27 games with three ties and only four losses. That was one of the best records in the country at the time.

In 1986, the season before Emmitt arrived, the Gators had barely been able to keep their heads above water. They had a 6–5 record and were seventh in the Southeastern Conference (SEC). They had a strong passing game, but their rushing offense ranked last in the league.

The star of the team was senior quarterback, Kerwin Bell. A lot of people thought Kerwin had a chance to win the Heisman Trophy. (The Heisman has been awarded every year since 1935 to the best college football player in the United States.) Kerwin was so popular that the university set up a weekly conference call for him to talk to the press. Every Wednesday, newspaper and magazine writers around the country talked to Kerwin.

Many of the other positions on the Gator football team were filled with younger, less experienced players. Emmitt was the team's third-string running back. Florida's coach, Galen Hall, didn't realize how good this freshman could be. When the season began, the coaches were still trying to sort things out.

In their first game of the season, the Gators played the University of Miami. Miami had played for the national championship the year before in the Fiesta Bowl, versus Penn State University. Emmitt didn't play much, and the Gators lost, 31-4. Florida's next opponent, the University of Tulsa, wasn't expected to be as tough. Coach Hall planned to give most of his running backs playing time.

Emmitt got his chance in the second period and he made the most it. With Florida ahead 3–0, he took a handoff from the quarterback and busted through the line of scrimmage. Before anyone could blink, Emmitt had run 66 yards for a touchdown! He rushed for a total of 109 yards for the game. Florida won, 52–0!

Coach Hall still wasn't sure that an 18-year-old freshman could be his full-time running back. But his team needed a strong running game, so he decided to give Emmitt a chance to start. Florida's next opponent was the University of Alabama. Alabama was one of the best teams in the SEC. Florida hadn't beaten the Crimson Tide, as the Alabama football team was known, since 1963.

Coach Hall was prepared to replace Emmitt if he failed, but the freshman stole the show once again. He carried the ball 39 times for 224 yards and two touchdowns. The Gators won, 23–14!

Emmitt's 224 yards were the most ever by a running back at Florida. In just his third college game, he had broken a school record that had stood since 1930!

The head coach for Alabama, Bill Curry, could hardly believe how good Emmitt was. He could tell that Emmitt's big game had not just been beginner's luck. "You can't practice the way he runs," Coach Curry said after the game. "It's a God-given talent."

Coach Curry wasn't the only one who realized that Emmitt was going to be a star. Another running back at Florida, Octavius "Liquid" Gould, also knew it. Octavius had been a high school All-America, and had led the Gators in rushing as a freshman, in 1986. But when he saw Emmitt zigging and zagging through the Alabama defense, he knew Florida's offense wasn't big enough for the two of them. He decided to transfer to the University of Minnesota.

Emmitt felt bad that his teammate was leaving. "I tried to convince him to stay," Emmitt said. "I told him we'd need more than one tailback. But he made it clear he was transferring because of me."

After the Alabama game, Emmitt kept running through, around, and over the opposition. He gained 173 yards against Mississippi State, in a 38–3 Florida win. He gained 184 yards against Louisiana State, in a tough 13–10 defeat. He racked up 130 yards against Cal State-Fullerton, in a 65–0 Gator chomp. And he totaled 175 yards in a 34–3 victory over Temple.

The win over Temple was the seventh game of the season. Florida had won five of them. Emmitt already had rushed for more than 1,000 yards. No freshman in college football history had ever gained 1,000 yards so quickly!

"We expected he was going to be good," Coach Hall said about Emmitt, "but we never expected those kinds of numbers that fast."

Now the secret was out. The college football world wanted to know more about this freshman running back at the University of Florida.

Reporters called Kerwin Bell on his weekly conference call to ask about Emmitt! "He's a natural," Kerwin told them. But the reporters wanted to hear it from Emmitt himself. So Emmitt and Kerwin started doing the weekly call together.

Emmitt was very mature for a college freshman. He didn't mind talking to reporters, even though it took up a lot of his free time. He talked about his teammates and how he thought the success of the team was more important than his own success.

Many reporters asked him about his chances of winning the Heisman Trophy. The Heisman almost always goes to a senior. No player in his first or second year has ever won the award.

Some people thought Emmitt had a chance to win it as a freshman. Emmitt didn't like to brag, but he did have a lot of confidence in himself. He wanted to be the best. When asked if he wanted to win the Heisman Trophy, he told reporters he wanted to win it "two, maybe three years in a row." (Only one player, Archie Griffin of Ohio State, has won the Heisman Trophy twice.)

Only one freshman had ever finished in the top 10 of the Heisman voting. (The voting is done by former Heisman winners and by reporters who cover college football.) That was Herschel Walker, of the University of Georgia. He finished third in 19tk. Two years later, Herschel, who is also a running back, won the Heisman Trophy. (He is now in the NFL, with the New York Giants.)

With the season winding down, Emmitt was closing in on Herschel's record for most rushing yards by a freshman. Florida had a chance to win the SEC Championship and go to the Sugar Bowl. The Sugar Bowl (along with the Rose Bowl, the Cotton Bowl, the Orange Bowl, and the Fiesta Bowl) is one of the most important post-season bowl games. But the Gators still had to play Auburn University (of Alabama) and the University of Georgia, two of the toughest teams on the schedule.

The Auburn Tigers and the Georgia Bulldogs were just too tough for the Gators. In the Auburn game, Emmitt gained only 72 yards. It was the first time since his sophomore year of high school that Emmitt had started a game and didn't gain at least 100 yards. He had an even tougher time against Georgia, Herschel's old school. In that game, Emmitt gained just 46 yards rushing on 13 carries. (He also had four receptions for 35 yards.) Florida lost both games.

The Gators finished their season at 6–5. Emmitt finished his season with 1,341 yards. It wasn't enough to break Herschel's record, but it was the most yards ever by a freshman at the University of Florida. Emmitt finished ninth in the Heisman Trophy voting. He was also given honorable mention on the Associated Press All-America team. He had gone from a third-string running back on his own team to one of the top running backs in the country, and he was still just a freshman!

Although they didn't make the Sugar Bowl, the

Gators were invited to another bowl game after the regular season. They played the University of California at Los Angeles (UCLA) in the Aloha Bowl in Hawaii. Emmitt played a great game, rushing for 128 yards. But Florida lost, 20–16. UCLA was led by a quarterback named Troy Aikman. This was the only time that Emmitt and Troy ever played against each other. Little did they know that they would someday be teammates in the NFL.

HEAD TO HEAD

While Emmitt was chasing records as a freshman at the University of Florida in 1987, Barry Sanders was a backup running back at Oklahoma State University. Barry led the nation in returning kicks that season. He earned first-team All-America honors from *The Sporting News* at that position. One year later, Barry would be his team's starting running back.

SEE YOU LATER, GATORS

Could Emmitt top last season? That's what Florida fans wondered when the 1988 season began. Emmitt had already broken a few school records and become one of the best running backs in the country. He had proven the critics wrong, and he had played only one season!

Emmitt was not about to sit back and relax. He thought it was great to have been in the running for the Heisman Trophy, but this year he wanted to win it. He wanted to be known as the best player in college football.

He picked up in 1988 right where he left off in 1987. He rushed for more than 100 yards in each of Florida's first five games. The Gators won all five.

Emmitt had already rushed for more than 2,000 yards in his college career. Only one player in college football history had ever reached the 2,000-yard mark faster — Herschel Walker. Once again, Emmitt and Herschel were linked together.

Herschel was one of the greatest running backs in

college football history. Emmitt was on track to join him in that fast company, but that is where their similarities ended. Emmitt wasn't as big as Herschel, or as fast. Herschel was 6' 1" tall, 225 pounds. He had been a world class sprinter. Emmitt was 5' 10", 205 pounds. He was not considered a very fast running back.

Emmitt did have a skill that very few running backs have — great vision. He could line up in the backfield and see the entire defense — not just the players right in front of him, but players lined up on the outside, too.

"It's not a blur, but a clear picture," Emmitt explained. "I see things other people don't see. I can see changes in coverage. I can look at a defense and see where the hole will be, regardless of where the play was called."

Just when teams were beginning to accept the fact that Emmitt was unstoppable, Emmitt was stopped. In a game against Memphis State University, Emmitt was hit in the back of the knee on a tackle. He suffered a stretched ligament in his knee. (Ligaments are elastic tissue that connect the bones of joints together.) The injury forced Emmitt to the sidelines.

It was the first major injury of Emmitt's career. It made him think: What if the injury were serious and I could never play football again?

Emmitt's parents and his high school coach had always told him that a football career could end at any

moment, and that's why a person's education is so important. So while Emmitt was recovering from the injury, he
made sure to study hard. Instead of traveling with the team
to away games, Emmitt stayed on campus to study.

With Emmitt out of action, the Gators had lost their
best offensive weapon. They lost the Memphis
State game. They then lost their next two games, to
Vanderbilt University and Auburn. The injury also cost
Emmitt his chance to win the Heisman.

Emmitt returned to the lineup for a game against the
University of Georgia. He was a little rusty from being out,
and ran for 68 yards on 19 carries. The Gators lost to the
tough Bulldogs, 26–3.

The next week, against the University of Kentucky,
Emmitt was in better form. He rushed for 113 yards, as
Florida squeaked by with a 24–19 win. Then the Gators had
their annual showdown with their in-state rival, Florida
State University. The FSU Seminoles, who were aiming for
the national championship, were just too tough. They ate
up the Gators, 52–17, and held Emmitt to just 56 yards.

The Gators finished the season with a record of 6–5
ck. But they were 6–0 in the games in which Emmitt had
rushed for at least 100 yards.

Florida was invited to play in the All-American Bowl
against the University of Illinois after the regular season.
Against Illinois, which plays in the Big 10 Conference,

Emmitt ran for 159 yards and scored two touchdowns. He led the Gators to a 14–10 victory. Once again, Emmitt's running made the difference for Florida. He was named the game's Most Valuable Player.

If he had not been injured, Emmitt might have rushed for more than 1,000 yards in 1988. Even after missing two games and playing while hurt late in the season, he still finished with 988 yards, 12 yards short of 1,000. But 1,000 yards rushing still would not have been enough for Emmitt to win the Heisman. At Oklahoma State University, a little-known running back had broken the all-time record for rushing yards in a season. He rushed for an amazing 2,628 yards and won the Heisman Trophy in a landslide vote. His name was Barry Sanders.

Many people believed that Emmitt and Barry were two of the best running backs in college football, and that one of them probably would win the Heisman in 1989. But Barry, who would have been a senior, decided to skip his final year of college and go to the NFL. With Barry in the NFL (he was a first-round draft pick of the Detroit Lions), Emmitt's chances of winning the Heisman Trophy were great.

Emmitt began the new college football season with a bang. He rushed for more than 100 yards in four of Florida's first five games. That included a 182-yard performance against Memphis State, the team he had gotten hurt against the season before. Then he did even better.

In the sixth game of the season, a 34–11 win over Vanderbilt, Emmitt gained 202 yards. A week later, on October 21, Emmitt had his best game ever. He carried the ball 31 times against the University of New Mexico, and rushed for a school-record 316 yards! The Gators won, 27–21, and Emmitt scored three touchdowns.

The game gave him a total of 3,457 yards for his college career, making him Florida's all-time rushing leader. Two months into the season, Emmitt was also leading the nation in rushing!

But then the Gators' season began to fall apart. The trouble started off the field. The starting quarterback, Kyle Morris, was kicked off the team because he was suspected of gambling. Coach Hall was having his own problems. He was being investigated by the National Collegiate Athletic Association (NCAA), which oversees college sports.

The NCAA believed Coach Hall was paying his assistant coaches money in addition to their salaries. That is against the NCAA rules. Midway through the season, Coach Hall resigned. But the NCAA continued to investigate the Florida football program to see if there was cheating going on in other areas.

Emmitt had had nothing to do with creating the problems at the University of Florida. But all the attention placed on the investigation was very distracting for him. "This has been a crazy year," Emmitt told reporters at the time. "I have to keep my mind on football."

That turned out to be a tough task for everyone on the Florida football team. Florida lost three of its last four games. They finished their season at 7–4. They were invited to play in the Freedom Bowl against the University of Washington. The Washington Huskies crushed the Gators, 34–7, and held Emmitt to only 17 yards.

Emmitt finished third in the nation in rushing and seventh in voting for the Heisman Trophy. He was a unanimous pick for the All-America team. But, all in all, it turned out to be a disappointing season.

There was always next season. Emmitt was still only a junior. But there was concern that Florida might be punished for breaking NCAA rules. If that happened, the Gators would not be allowed to compete for the conference championship next season. They could play, but their games wouldn't count in the standings.

Emmitt thought about skipping his senior year and entering the NFL draft, as Barry Sanders had done the year before. Getting his college diploma meant a lot to Emmitt and his family. But why risk possible career-ending injuries in games that didn't count? Emmitt knew that if he went to the NFL he could play football and make millions of dollars.

It was a tough decision. Emmitt's mother reminded him about the days at Escambia High when he told kids not to drop out of school. "How can you go around telling kids to stay in school if you didn't stay yourself?" she asked.

Emmitt and his mom made a deal. He would leave the University of Florida and go to the NFL, but he would return to school during the offseason.

In his three years at Florida, Emmitt set 58 school records, including ones for most rushing yards in a career (3,928), most yards in a season (1,599 yards in 1989), and most yards in one game (316 yards against the University of New Mexico in 1989). The career rushing record was broken in 1993 by Errict Rhett, who did it in four years. Errict now plays for the Tampa Bay Buccaneers.

On January 31, 1990, Emmitt made the announcement that he was leaving Florida to enter the NFL Draft. "This is the opportunity of a lifetime," he said of his chance to join the NFL.

He did not win the Heisman Trophy, as he had hoped, but he still would go down in history as one of the best running backs in college football.

HEAD TO HEAD

Emmitt is just one of many University of Florida football players who went on to become NFL stars. They include: wide receiver Wes Chandler (New Orleans Saints and San Diego Chargers), wide receiver Cris Collinsworth (Cincinnati Bengals), linebacker, and defensive end Jack Youngblood (Los Angeles Rams).

5
AMERICA'S TEAM

Emmitt Smith is too small to make it in pro football. Emmitt had heard that message a lot. But now, as the 1990 NFL draft approached, he was hearing it from people who scouted for the pros. Even though Emmitt weighed 209 pounds, he was just 5' 9 ½" tall.

Jimmy Johnson knew that bigger isn't always better. He was the head coach of the Dallas Cowboys. When he took over the team, in 1989, the Cowboys were struggling. In his first season, they finished with the worst record in the league, 1–15. Dallas needed a top-notch running back to help the offense. Coach Johnson heard what other NFL scouts were saying about Emmitt's size. But he decided to listen to what his own coaching staff had to say.

A Cowboy coach had visited Emmitt when he played at the University of Florida. He learned more about Emmitt than just his height and weight. It didn't matter that Emmitt was too small to run *over* defenders. The Cowboys knew he had a great talent for running around, through, and away from them! The Cowboys also learned that Emmitt didn't get bothered by bumps or bruises, that he was a hard worker, and he never complained. Coach Johnson had been the head football coach at the University of Miami before he came to the Cowboys. He had tried to recruit Emmitt for Miami when the running back was in high school. He knew the type of heart that Emmitt had.

Coach Johnson wanted Emmitt to be a Cowboy. The only problem was that the Cowboys could not make a selection until the 21st pick in the draft. The New England Patriots and the Green Bay Packers each had two picks in the first 20, so 18 teams would would have a chance to take Emmitt before the Cowboys did.

The NFL draft took place in April in New York City. Fans around the country watched the event on cable television. Team officials made their decisions about who they would draft, while also trying to make their teams better through trades. One by one, they gave the NFL commissioner, Paul Tagliabue, their pick. The commissioner then announced each team's selection.

After 16 selections had been made, Emmitt was still available. But Coach Johnson was getting worried. The Pittsburgh Steelers had the next pick. Before the Steelers used their pick, the Cowboys offered to make a deal with them. Dallas would give Pittsburgh an extra pick later in the draft if they would switch first-round spots with the Cowboys. The Steelers agreed and the Cowboys moved up in line, with the 17th pick in the draft.

Meanwhile, Emmitt himself was watching the draft on television at a friend's house on Pensacola Beach. Friends and some family members were watching with him. After the first ten players were picked, Emmitt couldn't watch any more. He was just too nervous.

He left the house to go outside and think. He was wondering if he would be drafted at all. Had he made a mistake by leaving school early? While he was outside, the phone rang. His mom called him into the house. The Dallas Cowboys' director of player personnel was on the phone.

He asked, "Emmitt, how would you like to be a Dallas Cowboy?" Emmitt said "I'd love to be a Dallas Cowboy." Emmitt gave the man his agent's phone number. The man said he'd get back to him.

Five minutes later, the phone rang again. This time it was Cowboys coach Jimmy Johnson. He asked Emmitt if he wanted to wear a star on his helmet. (A star is the symbol of the Cowboys.) When Emmitt said yes, Coach Johnson said, "Good, because we're about to draft you. We want you in Dallas tonight."

Emmitt told everyone there that the Cowboys were going to draft him. His friends and family went crazy, screaming, hugging each other, laughing and crying.

On TV, NFL commissioner Paul Tagliabue made the announcement. "With the 17th pick in the 1990 NFL Draft, Dallas selected Emmitt Smith, running back, University of Florida." Emmitt was so happy he was shaking.

That night in Dallas, Emmitt met with reporters. He told them that he hoped to help the Cowboys return to their winning ways. He was so excited to be a Cowboy! The Dallas coaches were excited, too.

"Emmitt Smith will take your breath away," running backs coach Joe Brodsky said to reporters. "You might not get it back until he scores."

Later, Emmitt went to Texas Stadium, where the Cowboys play. He had seen the stadium on TV so many times. Many of the greatest players in football had played here. For years, the Cowboys were almost unbeatable in this building. This was the home field of his hero, Tony Dorsett. Now he was right there, on the field!

He looked up at the Cowboys' Ring of Honor. It's a list of the members of the Cowboys' Hall of Fame. Each member of the Ring of Honor has a star with his uniform number painted in it outside the press level. The stars circle the inside of the stadium. "One day," Emmitt said to himself, "I'll have my name with those other legends up there."

Emmitt couldn't wait to get to training camp and start his rookie season. But first he had to sign a contract. Emmitt's agent and Cowboy officials were trying to reach an agreement. But by the time training camp opened, in mid-July, they still hadn't worked out a deal.

Without a contract, Emmitt could not practice with

the team. He wanted to play and worried about missing practice time. But he remembered that Barry Sanders had had the same problem in 1989. Barry didn't sign his contract until three days before the season began. Then he went on to become the NFL's Offensive Rookie of the Year.

So Emmitt waited. He studied the team's playbook, memorizing the dozens of plays that the Cowboy offense runs. He needed to learn what his job was on every play, whether he was supposed to run with the ball, catch a pass, block a defender, or just be a decoy. He also worked out at the Escambia High field to stay in shape. Finally Emmitt signed a contract five days before the 1990 season began. He would earn three million dollars over three years.

Emmitt missed training camp, but after all of his hard work, he was ready to play. By the second week of the season, he was the Dallas Cowboys' starting running back.

The Cowboys weren't expected to make the playoffs in 1990. They had won only one game in 1989 and had an inexperienced team. But their talent was starting to show.

In 1988, Dallas had drafted wide receiver Michael Irvin. In 1989, the Cowboys had the first pick overall in the draft and had taken Troy Aikman, the UCLA quarterback who had beaten Emmitt and the Gators back in 1987. With Troy, Michael, and Emmitt in the offense, the Cowboys' future seemed bright.

After 10 games in 1990, the Cowboys were 3–7. Not

great, but that was still two more wins than they had had the entire season before. Emmitt was playing well, but he was frustrated. Like all great running backs, he needs to carry the ball a lot to get into the flow of a game. His muscles get looser and his senses get keener as he plays. Plus, he learns what defenders do in different situations and then puts that knowledge to work.

In college, Emmitt would carry the ball more than 20 times a game. But with the Cowboys, he was lucky if he got the ball 15 times. Because he was a rookie, and had missed training camp, the Dallas coaches were working him in a little bit at a time. He asked them to let him carry the ball more often. They granted his wish.

The coaches were glad they listened to Emmitt. With him running more, the Cowboys won four straight games. Emmitt ran with the ball 21 times for 54 yards, as the Cowboys beat the Rams, 24–21. The next week, Emmitt carried the ball 23 times for 132 yards to help the Cowboys beat the Redskins. He ran for 85 yards in a win over New Orleans, and 103 yards in a 41–10 win over Phoenix.

The Cowboys finished the season with a 7–9 record. Emmitt finished the season with 937 yards rushing and 11 touchdowns. Like Barry Sanders the year before, Emmitt was named NFL Offensive Rookie of the Year.

When the 1991 season began, Emmitt had big goals. He wanted to run for 1,500 to 2,000 yards, lead the NFL in rushing, catch 30–40 passes, become league MVP, and take the Cowboys to the playoffs — maybe even to the Super Bowl! It had been five years since Dallas had had a winning record, so that would not be easy. Winning the rushing title wouldn't be easy either. That meant beating out Barry Sanders. Barry had won the title in 1990.

E mmitt and the Cowboys got off to a shaky start. After their first three games, they had a record of 1–2. The Cowboys had a lot of potential scoring weapons — with Emmitt running and quarterback Troy Aikman passing to wide receivers Michael Irvin and Alvin Harper and tight end Jay Novacek — but they all were getting shut down at one time or another in the early games.

There were some good signs, however. In week two, Emmitt had a 75-yard touchdown run against the Washington Redskins. In week four, he ran 60 yards for a score against the Phoenix Cardinals. Emmitt was also becoming a good receiver. Through the first four games of the season, Emmitt had 18 catches for an average of 4.5 catches per game. That made the Cowboys' offense even more dangerous.

By late October, the Cowboys had a winning record and were shooting for the playoffs. Dallas traveled to Detroit for a game with the Lions. Both teams were 5–2.

The Lion defense focused on stopping Emmitt. And the Cowboy defense did its best to stop their opponent's running back. Who was that? Barry Sanders! Barry carried the ball 21 times for just 55 yards, but he also caught a touchdown pass. Dallas fell behind early, and passed a lot to try and catch up. Emmitt carried the ball only 16 times, gaining 66 yards. It wasn't enough. Detroit won, 34–10.

As the season wound down, Emmitt and Barry were neck-and-neck for the NFL rushing lead. The Cowboys knew Emmitt could win the title if they got the ball to him often. In the last game of the regular season, Emmitt carried the ball 32 times for 160 yards. He finished the season with 1,563 yards. Barry finished with 1,548 yards. Emmitt was the 1991 NFL rushing champion! Besides winning the rushing title, he helped the Cowboys finish 11–5. They were headed to the playoffs!

The first playoff game of Emmitt's career was a wild card game. The Cowboys were up against the Chicago Bears, a team known for its solid defense. But it was Dallas' defense that held the Bears in check for most of the day. Emmitt rushed for 105 yards and scored one touchdown, helping the Cowboys beat the Bears, 17–13. It was the first time a running back had ever gained at least 100 yards in a playoff game against the Bears!

Now the Cowboys had to play in Detroit again. The Lions finished first in the NFC Central division. They would be hard to beat.

The game went a lot like the previous Cowboys-

Lions game had gone. The Cowboys fell behind early, and had to pass the ball a lot as they tried to come back. Emmitt ran for 80 yards on just 15 carries. Barry gained just 69 yards, but he also scored a touchdown. The Detroit defense held Emmitt and the Cowboys to less than 100 rushing yards total. The Lions won, 38-6.

It was the best Cowboy season since 1983, when they finished 12–4 and went to the playoffs. Emmitt had achieved some of his goals: He had won a rushing title and led the Cowboys into the playoffs. But he would not be satisfied until he and his teammates had Super Bowl rings.

HEAD TO HEAD

Since 1977, the year that Tony Dorsett joined the Cowboys, only four different players have led Dallas in rushing. Who are they? Tony led from 1977 to 1986. Herschel Walker led in 1987 and 1988. Paul Palmer led the team in 1989. And Emmitt has been the Cowboy's leading rusher each year since 1990.

6

THE NEW RUSHING CHAMP

The 1991 playoffs helped Emmitt and the Cowboys in a few ways. First, by winning a playoff game, they realized that they really were becoming a good team. By losing, they learned that they would have to work a lot harder in 1992 to reach their goal of making it to the Super Bowl. They weren't the only ones who thought they could be a special team. *Sports Illustrated* picked the Cowboys as a pre-season Super Bowl contender.

In the offseason, the Cowboys made some additions to help their defense. They added Pro Bowl defensive end Charles Haley in a trade with the San Francisco 49ers. They also drafted corner back Kevin Smith and linebacker Robert Jones. The offense was set with Emmitt and Daryl "Moose" Johnston at running back, Troy Aikman at quarterback, and Michael Irvin, Alvin Harper and Jay Novacek as the receivers.

The 1992 season started with a great test. The defending Super Bowl champions, the Washington

Redskins, came to Texas Stadium for a Monday night game. Emmitt scored the first Dallas touchdown of the season in the first quarter, on a five-yard run. For the game, he rushed for 140 yards on 27 carries. The Cowboys upset the NFL champions, 23–10.

The following week brought another test from the Super Bowl champions of two years earlier, the New York Giants. Midway through the third quarter, the Cowboys had built a 34–0 lead. Emmitt was having a solid game with 89 yards on the ground and eight catches for 55 yards. Then, suddenly, the Giants offense woke up. They scored four unanswered touchdowns. With under seven minutes remaining, New York trailed by only six points.

The Cowboy defense rose to the challenge. They stopped the Giants on their final possession to save the win. In two weeks, the Cowboys had beaten the past two Super Bowl champs! They were starting to believe in themselves.

After beating the Phoenix Cardinals in week three, the Cowboys had another big game. They had to travel to Philadelphia to face their bitter rivals, the Philadelphia Eagles. Emmitt described the Dallas-Philadelphia rivalry very simply: "My teammates and I hate the Philadelphia Eagles," he said.

This was a big game for both teams. Both had records of three wins and no losses. The winner would take sole possession of first place in the NFC East. It was also a big game for former Cowboy, then Eagle, Herschel Walker. Herschel had been traded by the Cowboys to the Minnesota Vikings the year before Emmitt arrived in Dallas. When he became a free agent, Herschel signed with the Eagles. This would be his first game against his former Dallas team.

The Eagles were ready for the Cowboys. Herschel scored two touchdowns and the Eagles held Emmitt to just 67 yards rushing. The Eagles won the game, 31–7, and took over first place.

The Cowboys were down, but they weren't out. They bounced back from their losses and went on a winning streak. In their next two games, Dallas defeated the Seattle Seahawks and the Kansas City Chiefs. After those wins, they went to Los Angeles to play the Raiders in the Los Angeles Memorial Coliseum. More than 91,000 fans watched Emmitt rush for 152 yards and three touchdowns in the Cowboys' 28–13 win. It was the largest crowd ever to watch the Cowboys or Emmitt play.

The following week was a rematch with the Eagles. Since their first matchup, the Cowboys had not lost. The Eagles had struggled, losing two out of the three games they had played since facing Dallas. Coach Johnson wanted the Cowboys to learn a lesson from the Eagles' troubles: To reach the Super Bowl, a team must not to lose its focus by getting too excited over a regular season win. Emmitt listened to the coach and rushed for 163 yards, including a 51-yard run to set up the go-ahead field goal in the Cowboys' 20–10 win.

Detroit was the next stop. The Cowboys were thinking about the two losses they suffered there in the past season. The last loss had sent the Cowboys home from the playoffs. This time the result was very different. Emmitt rushed for three touchdowns on only 67 yards. The Cowboy defense was able to keep the Lions from scoring a touchdown, even though Barry Sanders rushed for 108 yards. Dallas won, 37-3. The Cowboys were on a long winning streak, and they were very confident. They were also in first place in their division

Perhaps the Cowboys were too confident. The Los Angeles Rams came to Dallas with a 3–6 record. They held Emmitt to less than 100 yards rushing and stunned the Cowboys, 27–23.

No one expected this loss. The Dallas defense had only allowed 36 points in the last five games. Emmitt described the feeling of the team: "Our players knew we blew it against the Rams."

The loss to L.A. may have helped the Cowboys. Like the loss to the Eagles, it taught them a lesson. They learned not to take any team lightly. Any opponent could beat them if they didn't give their best effort in every game.

In the Cowboys' next game, against Phoenix, Emmitt made news again. It wasn't for his 84 rushing yards. It was for his career high 12 catches! Teams couldn't just focus on stopping Emmitt from running now; they also had to deal with him catching the ball out of the backfield.

It's a Cowboy tradition to host a game on Thanksgiving day. A rematch with the Giants was this year's game. This time the Cowboys built a big lead and held on to it. Emmitt scored two big touchdowns in the third quarter. On the first, he caught a short pass from Troy Aikman and ran 26 yards into the end zone. On the second, he broke loose for a 68-yard touchdown run.

With four games left in the regular season, the Cowboys held a three game lead in their division. They shared the best record in the NFC with the San Francisco 49ers, who were also 10–2. The team with the best record in the conference gets to be the home team throughout the playoffs, so it was important for the Cowboys to win the rest of their games.

After defeating the Denver Broncos in a close game, the Cowboys went to Washington, D.C. There they would face the champion Redskins again. The tie with the 49ers for best record would be broken with a dramatic game.

The Cowboys led, 17–13, late in the fourth quarter when Troy Aikman dropped back in his own end zone to pass. He was hit by defensive end Jason Buck of the

Redskins, who knocked the ball loose. Emmitt picked up the fumble. He should have fallen on the ball for a safety, which would have given the Redskins two points but kept the Cowboys ahead, 17–15. Instead, he tried throwing the ball upfield to a teammate. The ball hit a teammate's leg and was recovered in the end zone by the Redskins for a touchdown! Washington won, 20–17. It was the worst loss of the year and very embarrassing for Emmitt.

But Emmitt and the Cowboys came back in a big way against the Atlanta Falcons. Emmitt rushed for 174 yards, including two touchdown runs, in a 41–17 Dallas win.

Going into the last week of the season, Emmitt was in a close race for the rushing title. This time, instead of Barry Sanders, he was competing with another Barry — running back Barry Foster of the Pittsburgh Steelers.

Before their games started on Sunday, December 27, Barry led Emmitt by five yards. The Steelers were playing an early game against the Cleveland Browns. The Cowboys were playing late in the day against the Chicago Bears. Barry finished up the day with 103 yards rushing, for a season's total of 1,690 yards. The Steelers won the game and clinched the AFC Central title. Emmitt would have to rush for more than 108 yards against the Bears to be rushing leader again.

Early in the third quarter, Emmitt had already rushed for exactly 100 yards when he took a handoff and ran for 31 yards and a touchdown. The run made the score 10–0, and won the rushing title for Emmitt. The Cowboys won 27–14 to finish the season at 13–3. Emmitt finished with a new Cowboy record 1,713 yards rushing for the season and his second straight rushing title!

The playoffs began with the Cowboys facing their old "friends," the Philadelphia Eagles. (Because the Cowboys had won their division, they didn't have to play a wild-card game. Instead, they got a week off.) Though the Eagles had beaten the Cowboys earlier in the season, this game wasn't even close. Emmitt rushed for 114 yards to lead the Cowboys to a 34–10 win. The Cowboys now had to face the 49ers for the right to go to the Super Bowl.

The Niners were led by NFL MVP quarterback Steve Young and All-Pro receiver Jerry Rice. The game would be held in San Francisco because the 49ers had the best record in the NFC (14–2). This didn't seem to bother the Cowboys or Emmitt. Emmitt ran for 114 yards for the second straight game. The Cowboys won, 30–20. They were one step away from reaching their ultimate goal . . . winning the Super Bowl.

The Super Bowl was played in the Rose Bowl stadium in Pasadena, California. It's the same place where Emmitt had watched Super Bowl XXI when he was in high school and had promised himself that he would play in the

Super Bowl some day. He had kept his promise! Emmitt would also be the first-ever NFL rushing champion to play in the Super Bowl.

The Cowboys would face the AFC champion Buffalo Bills. The Bills were led by quarterback Jim Kelly, running back Thurman Thomas, and a defense led by All-Pro defensive end Bruce Smith. Buffalo had been to the Super Bowl in the past two seasons. They had been beaten by the New York Giants and by the Washington Redskins.

The Bills' Super Bowl experience showed early in the game. They jumped out to a 7–0 lead, scoring early in the first quarter. If the Cowboys weren't ready, they might have cracked then. But late in the first quarter, the Cowboys came right back. Troy Aikman threw a 23-yard pass to tight end Jay Novacek. Touchdown!

On Buffalo's next play, quarterback Jim Kelly was sacked near his own end zone and fumbled. Cowboy defensive lineman Jimmie Jones picked up the ball. He ran two yards and scored Dallas' second touchdown.

The Bills scored a field goal to make the score 14–10. But Michael Irvin caught two touchdown passes from Troy and the Cowboys had a 28-10 lead at halftime.

The Bills scored a touchdown in the third quarter after the Cowboys kicked another field goal to make it 31–17 going into the fourth quarter. In the fourth, Emmitt took a handoff and sprinted 10 yards into the end zone for his first Super Bowl touchdown. On that day he rushed for

108 yards. He also caught six passes for 27 more yards.

Emmitt wasn't the biggest star of the game. Troy was named MVP and the Cowboy defense had forced the Bills into many fumbles and interceptions. The Cowboys won the game, 52–17! They were Super Bowl champions. Emmitt had reached his ultimate goal.

HEAD TO HEAD

Emmitt never collected sports cards as a kid. But he started a collection when he joined the NFL. He liked collecting so much, he opened up a store called Emmitt Inc. Trading Cards and Collectibles. His family helps him run the business — but Emmitt pitches in whenever he can.

7
TENSION AND TRIUMPH

E mmitt Smith was now known as one of the best running backs in the NFL. He had won back-to-back rushing titles and helped lead the Cowboys to a Super Bowl title. He was on top of the world.

When the Super Bowl celebrations died down, Emmitt went back to Florida. He took some classes at the University of Florida and spent time resting up at his parents' house. While in Pensacola, Emmitt stayed in the same bedroom he slept in as a kid. He also kept busy making ads for magazines and TV.

Emmitt was enjoying himself, but tension was growing back in Dallas. It was time for Emmitt to sign a new contract. Once again, his agent Richard Howell and Cowboy owner Jerry Jones could not agree.

Even though Emmitt didn't have a contract, he attended the Cowboys' offseason workouts. In July, the Cowboys started training camp. They were preparing to make another run for the Super Bowl. Emmitt wasn't at camp. He would not report until he got a new contract.

While his teammates practiced in Texas, Emmitt was

in Pensacola. During the mornings, he trained at Escambia High School. He would sprint on the track and run up hills. He also played golf and spent time working at his sports collectibles store in Pensacola, Emmitt Inc.

What Emmitt really wanted to do was play football. He wanted the Cowboys to repeat as Super Bowl champs. And he wanted to win his third straight rushing title. That was something only three other players had ever done in the history of the NFL.

In September, when the 1993 NFL season was about to begin, Emmitt and the Cowboys still had not agreed on a contract. The Cowboys would have to start the season without Emmitt.

The Cowboys first game of the season was against the Washington Redskins, a team they had defeated the last time they faced them. Now, without Emmitt, Dallas lost the first game of the season to Washington, 35-16. The Cowboys would face the Bills in their second game. Eight months earlier, the Cowboys had crushed Buffalo in Super Bowl XXVII. But this time the Bills got revenge. They defeated the Cowboys, 13-10, in Texas Stadium. Derrick Lassic, the rookie running back who was playing in place of Emmitt, fumbled twice. The Bills scored 3 points as a result of the fumbles.

Cowboy owner Jerry Jones had seen enough. He knew the team needed Emmitt. He called his star running back's agent and offered him a four-year contract worth

13.6 million dollars. Emmitt accepted the deal, making him the highest-paid running back in the NFL. He packed his bags, hugged his family good-bye, and jumped on a plane to Dallas. Finally, Emmitt was back!

Was it too late? No team had ever started the season 0–2 and won the Super Bowl. And how could Emmitt win the rushing title after missing the first two games of the season? Emmitt wasn't worried. He was sure that he and the Cowboys could reach their goals. "It's not how you start," he said. "It's how you finish."

Emmitt signed his contract just three days before the Cowboys' third game of the season, against the Phoenix Cardinals (now the Arizona Cardinals). He was in uniform for the game. Although he had kept in shape during his holdout, it took him some time to get going. Midway through the third quarter, with the Cowboys leading 17–0, Emmitt got into the game. He responded by gaining 45 yards on eight carries (that's an average of almost six yards per carry)!

Derrick Lassic, who had struggled while trying to fill Emmitt's shoes, scored two touchdowns against the Cardinals. The Cowboys won, 17–10. Derrick knew that Emmitt's return meant that he would not get to play much anymore, but that was okay with him. Having Emmitt back lifted the spirits of his other teammates, too. It was "just like the good old days," said lineman Nate Newton. "When

Emmitt runs, you feel something powerful in there."

Emmitt gave the team a powerful jolt. With him back in the lineup, the Cowboys won seven games in a row!

On Halloween Day in 1993, the Cowboys played the Eagles in Philadelphia. It was a rainy day, but the bad weather couldn't slow Emmitt down. He was darting through the middle of the line and streaking outside for big gains on almost every play. By the fourth quarter, Emmitt had rushed for over 150 yards. But the Cowboys were only ahead by six points.

With four minutes to play and the Cowboys trying to run out the clock, Dallas called a draw play. Troy Aikman dropped back as if he were going to pass, then he handed the ball to Emmitt. The Cowboy fullback, Daryl "Moose" Johnston, threw a crushing block on an Eagle defender and Emmitt was gone. He ran 62 yards for the touchdown!

Emmitt finished the game with 237 yards. It was a team record and it tied Emmitt for the sixth-best rushing day in NFL history. It also helped him get closer to the NFL rushing lead.

He still had a long way to go to win his third straight rushing title. Barry Sanders of the Detroit Lions, the last player to win the title before Emmitt, was leading the league by just over 200 yards. But in a Thanksgiving Day game against the Chicago Bears, Barry hurt his left knee. He would be out for the rest of the season.

"I felt bad when I heard Barry Sanders went down," Emmitt said. "I don't like to see anybody get injured."

If Barry had not gotten hurt, he probably would have won the rushing title. But Barry's injury opened the door for Emmitt, who was closing in on the rushing crown.

With one game left to play in the season, Emmitt and Los Angeles Ram Jerome Bettis were battling for the rushing title. The Cowboys' last game was against the New York Giants. The winner would finish with the NFC's best record and have the home-field advantage throughout the playoffs. Emmitt suffered a shoulder injury just before halftime. Despite the pain, he played the game of his life. Emmitt carried the Cowboys on his shoulders — even though one of those shoulders was injured.

The Cowboys won, in overtime, 16–13. Emmitt totaled 168 yards rushing and another 61 yards receiving. He ended the regular season with 1,486 yards rushing — 57 yards more than Jerome Bettis. Emmitt was the rushing champ again!

Not only was he the league's top rusher, he was also named MVP of the regular season — even though he had missed the first two games!

But the job was not finished. Emmitt had achieved his individual goal, but his team goal was for the Cowboys to repeat as Super Bowl champs.

The Cowboys won both of their playoff games,

defeating the Green Bay Packers and the San Francisco
49ers. With that victory, they earned a trip to Super Bowl
XXVIII in Atlanta, Georgia. There they would face the
Buffalo Bills once again.

Buffalo had beaten Dallas earlier in the season, but
that was without Emmitt. Still, the Bills were confident.
They jumped out to a 13–6 lead at halftime.

The Cowboys had been trying to mix things up on
offense, giving Emmitt a rest. The shoulder he had injured
in the Giants game was not healed. But Emmitt knew what
the Cowboys had to do to win the game.

"Get the ball to me," Emmitt told the coaches in the
locker room at halftime. Offensive coordinator Norv Turner
asked Emmitt if he wanted the ball in a handoff or a pass.
"It doesn't matter," Emmitt said. "Just get me the ball."

The Cowboys came out in the second half and got
the ball to Emmitt. He did the rest. Emmitt scored two
touchdowns. His first was on a 15-yard run. It put the
Cowboys up 20–13. They would never trail again! His second touchdown, on a 1-yard run, made the score 27–13.

The Cowboys dominated the Bills, outscoring them
24–0 in the second half. Dallas won the Super Bowl, 30–13.
Emmitt finished with 132 yards rushing. He was named the
game's Most Valuable Player.

When the game was over, Emmitt thought about all
he and the Cowboys had accomplished that season. "I was
one of the last to leave the locker room after the game,"

Emmitt said. "This year's win felt even more special than last year's."

After the Super Bowl, Emmitt was on the cover of *Sports Illustrated.* The headline described Emmitt in one word: *Superman!*

HEAD TO HEAD

Emmitt is one of only four players in NFL history to win three straight rushing titles. The other players are all in the Pro Football Hall of Fame: Jim Brown of the Cleveland Browns, Steve Van Buren of the Philadelphia Eagles, and Earl Campbell of the Houston Oilers. Jim Brown holds the record with five straight seasons leading the NFL in rushing (1957–61).

8 CHASING LEGENDS

After all that Emmitt had achieved in his first four years, it's hard to believe that 16 players were taken ahead of him in the 1990 draft. Nobody would ever underestimate him again!

By the start of the 1994 season, the Cowboys were more popular than ever and Emmitt was one of the most famous athletes in the United States. How long could all this success continue?

The season began with two great quests. First, the Cowboys were trying to become the first team ever to win three Super Bowls in a row. And second, Emmitt was chasing after his fourth straight NFL rushing title. Only Hall of Fame running back Jim Brown had ever done that.

"That's awesome," Emmitt said of the chance to share a record with Jim Brown. "I want it!"

In March of 1994, doctors did surgery to repair Emmitt's separated right shoulder. By the time the 1994 season began, Emmitt was the same old Emmitt again. The Cowboys, however, were not the same as a team. Norv

Turner, who called the plays for the Cowboys offense, left Dallas to become head coach of the Washington Redskins. And head coach Jimmy Johnson, who had been having disagreements with Cowboy owner Jerry Jones, quit the team.

The team lost some key players, too. Linebacker Ken Norton, Jr., went to the San Francisco 49ers as a free agent. The Cowboys also lost Thomas Everett and Tony Casillas, who were the two other starters on defense. On offense, they lost guard Kevin Gogan and, midway through the season, they lost tackle Erik Williams. Erik, one of the NFL's best tackles, was seriously injured in a car crash.

The new head coach of the Dallas Cowboys was Barry Switzer. He had been a successful coach at the University of Oklahoma, but he had never been a coach in the NFL before.

All eyes were on Coach Switzer and the Cowboys as the 1994 season unfolded. The team got off to a good start, winning its first two games. First, the Cowboys beat the Pittsburgh Steelers, 26–9. Then, they defeated the Houston Oilers in a cross-state rivalry game, 20–17. Emmitt got off to a great start, too. He rushed for a total of 261 yards in just two games.

In the third game of the season, Emmitt and Barry faced each other for the fourth time in their pro careers. The Lions played Dallas in a Monday night game — and Barry and Emmitt put on quite a show for the national television audience.

Emmitt carried the ball 29 times for 143 yards and one touchdown. He also caught seven passes for another 49 yards. His touchdown tied the game, 17–17, with just over four minutes left to play. He also passed the 6,000 career yard mark in the game!

But Barry played better, and the Lions won the game in overtime, 20–17. In his first game ever in Texas Stadium, Barry carried the ball 40 times for 194 yards — the fourth-highest total ever against the Cowboys.

Emmitt continued to play well after the loss to Detroit, but he had a long way to go to catch Barry. Even after gaining 135 yards in a 38–10 win over the Giants in November, Emmitt trailed in the race for the rushing title. Emmitt carried the ball a career-high 35 times in that game. But he hurt himself in a game against the New Orleans Saints. He pulled his left hamstring (thigh muscle) and was forced to leave the game.

Emmitt missed the final game of the season because of his injury. He finished the season as the league's third-best rusher, with a total of 1,484 yards. Barry Sanders finished the season with 1,883 yards and the 1994 rushing title. Chris Warren of the Seattle Seahawks was second, with 1,545 yards.

Emmitt led the NFL in touchdowns for the season, with 22. He was selected to the Pro Bowl for the third straight time. His strong performance helped the Cowboys clinch first-place in their division.

Even though his left leg was still injured, Emmitt played in the NFC Championship Game. But when he injured his right hamstring late in the game, it was too much. He had to leave the game.

In the year when Emmitt's streak of rushing titles came to an end, so did the Cowboys' Super Bowl run. They lost to Steve Young and the 49ers in the NFC championship game. The 49ers went on to beat the San Diego Chargers in Super Bowl XXIX.

It was not the end of the world for Emmitt. It simply meant that he would come back in 1995 with more goals to achieve. He would try to take back the rushing title and get back to the Super Bowl.

So far, Emmitt has reached almost every goal he has set for himself. After the 1994 season, he went back to work on another long-time goal — finishing his college education (he plans to earn his degree by May, 1996). After class, he would practice on the football field, where his goals are endless.

When Emmitt's football career is over, he would like to continue in business. He would also like to get married and have children someday. Emmitt say it is very important to him "to love my kids the way my family loved me." He says he would never push his kids to play sports. But if they take after Emmitt, they probably will anyway!

EMMITT SMITH'S CAREER STATS

COLLEGE STATS University of Florida

	RUSHING				RECEIVING			SCORING
Season	Attempts	Yards	Avg.	TD	Rec.	Yards	TD	Points
1987	229	1,341	5.9	13	25	184	0	78
1988	187	988	5.3	9	10	72	0	54
1989	284	1,599	5.6	14	21	207	1	90
Totals	700	3,928	5.6	36	56	463	1	222

NFL STATS Dallas Cowboys

	RUSHING				RECEIVING			SCORING
Season	Attempts	Yards	Avg.	TD	Rec.	Yards	TD	Points
1990	241	937	3.9	11	24	228	0	66
1991	365*	1,583*	4.3	12	49	258	1	78
1992	373	1,713*	4.6	18*	59	335	1	114
1993	283	1,486*	5.3*	9	57	414	1	6
1994	368	1,484	4.0	21	50	341	1	132*
Totals	1,630	7,203	4.4	71	239	1,576	4	450

PLAYOFFS								
1991	41	185	4.5	1	1	2	2	0
1992	71	336	4.7	3	13	86	18	1
1993	66	280	4.2	3	13	138	28	1
1994	27	118	4.4	3	4	8	5	0
Totals	205	919	4.5	10	31	234	28	2

* led league

Emmitt Smith led the league in touchdowns in 1992 with 19 TD's and in 1994 with 22 TD's.

Emmitt is the third-leading high school rusher of all time. In college (left), at the University of Florida, he set 58 school records.

Emmitt's dream is to be the greatest rusher of all time. To do that, he'll have to top Walter Payton's career total of 16,726 yards.

Louis DeLuca

Emmitt led
the Cowboys
to Super Bowl
championships
after the 1992
and 1993 sea-
sons. He was
MVP of Super
Bowl XXVIII!

Emmitt owns a
sports collec-
tables store in
his hometown.
It's called
Emmitt Inc.
(That's his
mom and dad
standing next
to him.)

Peter Read Miller/Sports Illustrated

BARRY SPENT MOST OF HIGH SCHOOL PLAYING IN HIS BROTHER'S SHADOW. BYRON SANDERS WAS THE STARTING TAILBACK ON THE NORTH HIGH FOOTBALL TEAM. BARRY STARTED ONLY FIVE GAMES AT TAILBACK...

EMMITT WAS A STARTER ALL THROUGH HIGH SCHOOL, LEADING HIS TEAM TO TWO CHAMPIONSHIPS.